"Goodnight Hokies"

By Samantha Hawthorne

ISBN: 978-1-6943-2127-5

Goodnight

Hokies

There's a school that's known for excellence.

It's better than all the rest.

The Hokies never falter.

Virginia Tech is the best!

Hokies love to win, they never lose it.

It's an honor and a privilege,
to be a Virginia Tech student.

They study to be doctors and lawyers,

musicians, and dancers.

They study hard for exams,

to learn all the answers.

But now, it's getting late.

It's time to say goodnight.

Goodnight, beautiful campus.

Goodnight, incoming freshmen.

Goodnight, Cassel.

Goodnight, student section.

Goodnight, homework.

Goodnight, tests.

Goodnight, Virginia Tech...

you are the best!

Goodnight, Mom. Goodnight, Dad.

One day, I too...

will be a Virginia Tech grad.

Goodnight, Hokies!

Made in the USA
Middletown, DE
18 December 2019